the CRitteR club

Ellie the Flower Girl

by Callie Barkley ♥ illustrated by Tracy Bishop

LITTLE SIMON
New York London Toronto Sydney New Delhi

LITTLE SIMON

An imprint of Simon & Schuster Children's Publishing Division · 1230 Avenue of the Americas, New York, New York 10020. First Little Simon paperback edition August 2016. Copyright © 2016 by Simon & Schuster, Inc. All rights reserved, including the right of reproduction in whole or in part in any form. LITTLE SIMON is a registered trademark of Simon & Schuster, Inc., and associated colophon is a trademark of Simon & Schuster, Inc. For information about special discounts for bulk purchases, please contact Simon & Schuster Special Sales at 1-866-506-1949 or business@simonandschuster.com. The Simon & Schuster Speakers Bureau can bring authors to your live event. For more information or to book an event contact the Simon & Schuster Speakers Bureau at 1-866-248-3049 or visit our website at www.simonspeakers.com. Designed by Laura Roode. The text of this book was set in ITC Stone Informal Std.
Manufactured in the United States of America 0716 FFG
10 9 8 7 6 5 4 3 2 1
Cataloging-in-Publication Data is available from the Library of Congress.
ISBN 978-1-4814-6719-3 (hc)
ISBN 978-1-4814-6718-6 (pbk)
ISBN 978-1-4814-6720-9 (eBook)

Table of Contents

Chapter 1

Wedding Bells

Ellie Mitchell hurried out to the school playground for the last ten minutes of recess. She found her friends Marion, Amy, and Liz at the swing set.

Marion was pushing Amy on one of the swings. "What took you so long?" Marion asked Ellie.

"I stayed behind to see the photos,"

Ellie explained. She gave Liz a push on the other swing.

Their teacher, Mrs. Sienna, had been at her daughter's wedding over the weekend. She had come back with lots of pictures. And Ellie had asked to see *all* of them.

"I've decided something," Ellie announced. "All I want in life is to be a *flower girl*!"

Liz laughed. "How come?" she asked.

Ellie gasped dramatically. "I mean, scattering the flower petals? No one else in the wedding gets to do that," she pointed out. "And the fancy dress! That might be the

very best part! The flower girl at Mrs. Sienna's daughter's wedding was wearing this *gorgeous* pink dress. It had these different layers of  pink and sparkly beads. And it totally  matched her shoes!"

"If I were ever a flower girl," Marion said, "I would want to design my *own* dress." Marion loved fashion design.

Amy shook her head. "I'd be

way too nervous to be a flower
girl. I know I'd trip or something.
Then it would be remembered for-
ever in photos!" She shivered at the
thought. Amy didn't love being the
center of attention.

Liz pumped her legs, trying to swing higher. "We went to my uncle's wedding last summer," she said. "Each bridesmaid's dress was a different color. It was so colorful! I think it's kind of boring when all the dresses match."

Ellie smiled. "You *do* love color," she said to Liz. Liz was an artist, after all!

"Speaking of color," Amy cried, "Ms. Sullivan said we could help paint the fence at The Critter Club after school today!"

The four friends had started the only animal rescue shelter in their town of Santa Vista. They had named it The Critter Club and it was located in their friend Ms. Sullivan's barn.

"Fun!" Ellie exclaimed. "It will give us something to do, since we don't have any animals to take care of right now."

Liz grinned. "Do we get to paint it *any* color we want?" she asked hopefully.

At dismissal time, Ellie's mom picked her up from school. They made a quick stop at home so Ellie could change into painting clothes. Then Mrs. Mitchell drove her over to The Critter Club.

On the way, Ellie told her mom about her day. "Mrs. Sienna's daughter got married!" she exclaimed.

"And I got to see all the pictures!"

Ellie's mom smiled at her in the rearview mirror.

"If you thought that was exciting," Mrs. Mitchell said, "you must be really excited about your cousin Hailey's wedding in a few weeks."

Ellie gasped. "That's right!" she cried.

Mrs. Mitchell laughed. "Did you forget?"

Ellie laughed too. "I guess so! I wonder who *her* flower girls are," she said.

chapter 2

Puppy Love

Mrs. Mitchell dropped Ellie off outside the barn. Ellie ran inside. Liz, Marion, and Amy were already there. So was Amy's mom, Dr. Melanie Purvis, who was a veterinarian. She often helped the girls take care of their Critter Club animals.

They were all crowded around a

small animal crate. Dr. Purvis was reaching inside.

"Oh good!" Amy cried, seeing Ellie come in. "You're here!"

"Ellie," exclaimed Liz, "wait till you see our new guest!"

"Ohhh, who is it?" Ellie asked eagerly.

Dr. Purvis turned around. Cradled in her arms was one of the sweetest little puppies Ellie had ever seen!

"Awwwww," the girls all said together.

"She's a French bulldog," Dr. Purvis told them.

Ellie pet the puppy's neck. "I love her droopy cheeks!" she said. "She's so adorable!" Suddenly, the puppy licked Ellie's hand.

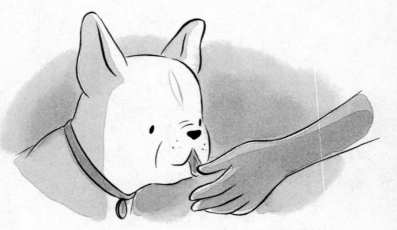

"Her name is Lulu," Dr. Purvis said. She explained that an elderly lady had brought Lulu in to the vet clinic. "Her grandchildren gave her

the puppy as a gift. But she was finding it hard to take care of Lulu properly."

Ellie nodded. It wasn't the best idea to give pets as surprise gifts. It often didn't work out.

"Well, Lulu," Ellie said, "I don't

think we'll have any trouble finding *you* a new home."

The other girls agreed. "Who
could resist that face?" Liz said.

Just then, they heard a knock at
the barn door. They turned to see a
young woman in the open doorway.
"Ellie?" she said, peering inside.

"Hailey!" Ellie cried, running over.
She gave the woman a big hug, then
turned. "Hey everyone, this is my
cousin Hailey!"

"Hello!" Hailey called out, waving.
"Sorry to drop in," she said to Ellie. "I
was just talking to your mom on the

phone. I was going to stop by your house to ask you and Toby about something. But she said you were here."

"I'm so glad you came!" Ellie said. She hadn't seen Hailey since last year at a family Christmas

party. One by one, she introduced Hailey to Amy, Marion, and Liz, and to Dr. Purvis.

"And this," Dr. Purvis said, "is Lulu!"

She held the puppy out. Hailey immediately reached out to pet her.

"Oh my gosh," she cooed. "I *love* French bulldogs! Awww . . ." Hailey looked at Dr. Purvis. "Do you think I could hold her?"

Dr. Purvis smiled. "Of course!" she said, handing Lulu to Hailey.

Hailey beamed as she cuddled Lulu. Lulu looked just as happy, covering Hailey's face with wet kisses.

"This is exactly the type of puppy I've always wanted," Hailey said.

Ellie and the girls looked at one another. Was their search for a new home for Lulu already over?

Chapter 3

Hailey Pops the Question

"You know, Hailey," Ellie hinted, "Lulu *is* up for adoption. That's why she's here at The Critter Club."

Hailey's smile faded. She sighed and handed Lulu back to Dr. Purvis. "I wish I could!" she said. "But I'd have to get Connor to agree. And we have a lot going on right now—including our wedding!"

She looked Ellie right in the eyes. "Speaking of which . . . ," Hailey continued. Now her face looked quite serious. "Ellie, I need to ask you something. It's something very important. Could we talk outside for a moment?"

Ellie nodded, feeling a pang of nervousness.

What was so important that she needed to ask Ellie . . . in private?

The next moments were a blur to Ellie. She followed Hailey out of the barn. She sat down next to her on the bench by the maple tree.

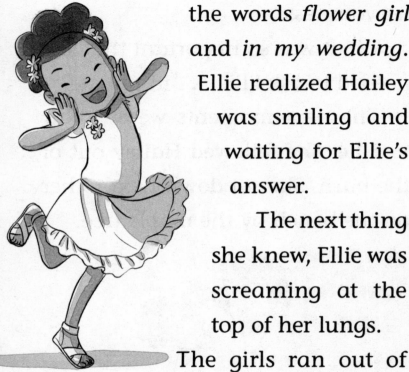

Then she heard the words *flower girl* and *in my wedding*. Ellie realized Hailey was smiling and waiting for Ellie's answer.

The next thing she knew, Ellie was screaming at the top of her lungs. The girls ran out of the barn. "Is everything okay?" Amy asked.

Ellie laughed and shouted,

"Hailey asked me to be the flower girl in her wedding! Whoo-hoooo!"

Amy, Liz, and Marion cheered. They gathered around Ellie and Hailey.

"Well? What did you say, Ellie?" Liz asked jokingly.

Ellie laughed. "I said yes, of course! Oh, I'm sooooo excited, Hailey."

"*I'm* so excited you said yes!" Hailey replied. "Next weekend, you can come with me to the bridal shop. I'll show you the flower girl dress I had in mind."

Ellie jumped up and down. "I can't wait!" she exclaimed.

Hailey stayed to play with Lulu for a while. She sat down with the girls in a circle on the grass. They let Lulu run around in the middle. When the puppy got tired, she flopped down between Hailey and Ellie. She put her head down on Hailey's leg.

Later on, at home, Toby met Ellie at the front door. "I'm going to be in Hailey's wedding!" he told Ellie. "I'm the ring bear! *Grrrrrr!*"

Ellie gave Toby a high five. "Awesome! But it's ring bear*er*," she explained. "You get to carry the wedding rings down the aisle. That's a big job!"

Toby stood up straight and looked very proud. For a split second, Ellie felt a pang of jealousy. *Wait a second,* she thought. *How come the flower girl doesn't get to deliver something important too?*

But Ellie shook it off. Toby would probably wear a tuxedo or a suit, not an awesome dress like hers.

Ellie couldn't wait to see what her flower girl dress looked like!

Chapter 4

Critter Club on the Case

On Friday after school, the girls met at The Critter Club. They filled Lulu's bowl with puppy food. Then they watched her gobble it down while they made plans to get her adopted.

Earlier in the week, they had put an ad in the newspaper. Amy's dad was an editor at *The Coastal County*

Courier. He got their ad a good spot in the Classifieds section.

But so far, they hadn't gotten any phone calls about Lulu.

"Well," said Amy, "we've found homes for lots of animals. Let's think. What has worked before?"

Ellie recalled the time she'd brought the bunnies on stage at the end of her play. "It definitely worked," she pointed out.

Marion remembered taking the stray kittens to a horse show. They found homes for all of them in one day!

Liz remembered the holiday party they threw to get

people to come meet two guinea pigs.

"So how can we get Lulu out to meet people?" Ellie wondered.

They were quiet as they thought it over. Then Amy spoke up.

"The weather is going to be nice this weekend," she said. "We could take Lulu on a field trip. Maybe to the park?"

Ellie, Marion, and Liz loved the

idea. There would be lots of people out. They could introduce Lulu around.

"Plus, I think Lulu will love it!" Amy said.

Lulu wagged her stubby tail and barked. *Arf, arf!*

It was decided. Amy and Marion would take Lulu to the park on Saturday. And Ellie and Liz would take her on Sunday.

"Perfect," said Ellie, "because I can't do it tomorrow. I have a big appointment at the bridal shop!"

Ellie sank into the floral print armchair. She looked around the dressing room of the bridal shop. It was the largest, fanciest dressing room she had ever been in.

Hailey was sitting next to her in a matching chair. "Can you just tell

me what *color* the flower girl dress is? Teal? Red? Pink?"

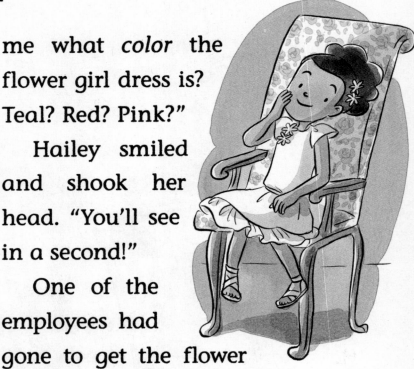

Hailey smiled and shook her head. "You'll see in a second!"

One of the employees had gone to get the flower girl dress Hailey had picked out. Ellie was going to try it on for size.

It was so hard to be patient. Seconds felt like minutes, which felt like hours.

"So how is little Miss Lulu?" Hailey asked while they waited. "Have you guys had any luck getting her adopted yet?"

Ellie shook her head distractedly. "Nope," she said, "not yet." She was listening for any sign of that employee coming back.

Finally, there were footsteps and the employee came back into the room. She handed Hailey a dress in a garment bag.

"Here it is, Ellie," Hailey said. "I hope you love it as much as I do!"

Ellie jumped out of her chair. She craned her neck to see as Hailey unzipped the garment bag. Ellie took the hanger. She held the dress against her body and looked in the mirror.

She took a long look . . . and her excitement slowly fizzled.

This is a flower girl dress? Ellie thought. There had to be some mistake.

This was a plain, straight lavender dress. It had no sleeves, a simple neckline, and no decorations or fancy details. Where was the sparkle? Where were the fabric rosettes?

Hailey was looking hopefully at Ellie and smiling. "Isn't it elegant? I think it's going to look amazing on you. But what do *you* think?"

Ellie hesitated. Hailey had picked out the dress. And Ellie really didn't want to hurt her feelings.

Ellie forced a smile. "I love it," she said.

Chapter 5

Lulu Goes on Tour

Ellie and Liz waited while Lulu stopped to sniff the grass along the park path. It was Sunday and they were taking their turn at "Operation Find Lulu a Home."

The day before, Amy, Marion, and Lulu had met a bunch of nice people in the park. They were all happy to meet the puppy. They

49

even agreed she was super adorable. But no one had been ready, willing, and able to adopt her.

Ellie and Liz decided they'd walk the looping path around the outside

of the park. As they walked, Ellie told Liz about the dress—and how she'd used her acting skills.

"I had to dig down deep," Ellie said dramatically. "But I think

Hailey believed me when I said I liked it."

Liz smiled. "It can't be that bad, can it?" she asked.

Ellie shrugged. "It's not *ugly*," she agreed. "It's a very nice lavender dress. And it fit me perfectly. They didn't have to hem it or anything, so I got to take it home. It's just . . . plain." Ellie sighed loudly. "I hoped it would have some pizzazz.

Some zing! Some star power!" She
looked at Liz.
"You know?"

Liz put her
arm around
Ellie. "I know,"
she said kindly.
"You do love
star power."

Ellie nodded.
"But what can
I do? Hailey picked that dress and
I'll just have to keep my opinion to
myself!"

They continued on the path

around the park. It took a while because there were so many people who stopped them to ask about Lulu.

"Oh my goodness! That's the most adorable puppy!" said a young lady jogging by.

"Is your puppy a boy or a girl?" asked a little boy who wanted to pet Lulu.

"How old is she?" asked the little boy's dad.

Even a woman selling flowers from a cart stopped them. "And what is this little munchkin's name?" she asked the girls.

They told everyone they talked to that they were trying to find Lulu a new home.

"Oh, Lulu," the flower seller said to the puppy. "If only I didn't already have a dog." She looked up at the girls. "A rather active dog. He doesn't play so well with others."

She was packing up her cart and getting ready to leave. She took three flowers out of one of her pails. "Here," she said, "take these. Three daisies for three young ladies." She gave one to Ellie. She gave one to Liz. And she tucked the third under Lulu's collar. Then she smiled and turned to go.

Ellie and Liz beamed. "Thank you!" they called after her.

The daisies were each a different vibrant color. "You look fabulous!" Ellie

said to Lulu. "So dressed up!"

They walked on, finishing their loop around the park. Then they took Lulu back to The Critter Club.

At home Ellie went up to her room. She sniffed her daisy as she

flopped down on her bed.

Hanging from her closet door was the flower girl dress. Ellie sighed. One little flower had really dressed Lulu up. "If only there were a way I could *dress up* that dress," she said to herself. "But I can't."

She looked at the flower in her hand. She looked up at the dress.

"Or can I?"

Dress Disaster!

Ellie went to her closet. She pulled out a box that held her belts. Her eyes were drawn to a glittery pink one.

In a flash, she changed out of her clothes and put on the flower girl dress. She couldn't reach the back zipper to zip it all the way up, but it was close enough.

Ellie added the pink belt around the waist. She checked her reflection in her mirror.

"Wow!" she said out loud. A little sparkle made a big difference.

Maybe she'd show Hailey the next time she saw her.

Ellie took off the belt and put it down on her bed. It landed next to the daisy.

All of a sudden, Ellie had an idea!

She pulled her craft bin out from under her bed and opened the lid. She tossed aside the bottles of paint

on top. Underneath, she found what she was looking for.

There were fabric flowers in different colors. There were glittering fake gems. There were shiny sequins and brightly colored beads.

Just think what a few details could do for this dress! Ellie thought. *A few flowers on one*

shoulder? A line of
beading around
the neckline?
A sprinkling of
sequins on the skirt?
Or maybe . . . Ellie gasped at the
picture she was painting
in her mind. *Maybe
all of that!*

Just then, Ellie heard her mom calling from downstairs. "Ellie! Dinner!"

"Coming!" Ellie called back.

Her mom's voice had snapped Ellie out of her daydream. She shook her head. There was no way she'd actually make any changes to the dress. First of all, she knew there was a big chance she'd mess it up!

And besides, what would I tell Hailey? Ellie thought. She picked up the glittery pink belt and put it away. She wasn't going to show it to Hailey after all.

Ellie looked at the dress in the mirror. She smiled. So it wasn't the

flower girl dress she had hoped for. But it *was* pretty. And Ellie *was* the flower girl. It was time to start getting excited!

Ellie gathered up the craft supplies she had taken out of the tub. She dumped everything back inside. She reached for the lid and put it on top. But it didn't click into place. Ellie pushed down hard, trying to force it closed.

"Why—isn't—this—closing," Ellie said as she kept trying to push the lid down. She tried again, putting all her weight on the lid.

SQUIIIIIIISSSSSHHHH! A jet of orange paint shot out from a bottle that had been wedged under the lid. It splattered all over the skirt of Ellie's dress.

"Oh no! Oh no! Oh no!" Ellie repeated over and over. She grabbed her pink towel from the back of her door. She used it to dab at the paint splotches. Instead of coming off, they smeared into one big splotch.

Ellie was panicking. Would the

paint wash out of fabric? What if it didn't? Had she just completely messed up the dress?

Had she wrecked Hailey's wedding?

Chapter 7

The Hard Truth

Ellie raced down to the kitchen.

"Mom!" she shouted, her voice shaking. "It's the worst thing ever!" She showed the paint splotch to her mom and told her what had happened. "What am I going to do?"

Mrs. Mitchell tried to calm Ellie down. "Okay, sweetheart," she said.

"First things first. Take a few deep breaths."

Ellie's mother knew about a trick using a kitchen knife to scrape any excess paint off the fabric. Ellie watched her give it a try. Afterward, the stain looked a little better. But it was still there.

"I'm not sure what to do next," Mrs. Mitchell said. "I think this might be oil-based paint. We'd need a strong cleaner to get it out." She felt the dress fabric. "But sometimes it damages the fabric."

Mrs. Mitchell looked Ellie straight

in the eye. "Honey," she said, "I hate to say this. But I think you need to call Hailey. Let her know what happened. Maybe a dry cleaner can clean the dress. But we should let Hailey decide what to do next."

Ellie felt a knot in the pit of her stomach. What her mom said made sense. But she really didn't want to tell Hailey. What would Hailey say? Would she be super mad?

Mrs. Mitchell dialed Hailey's number and handed Ellie the phone. It rang once, twice, three times.

Maybe she won't answer! Ellie silently hoped.

"If she doesn't answer, leave her a message," her mom said.

Ugh! thought Ellie.

Hailey's voice mail picked up. After the beep, Ellie took a deep breath.

"Hi, Hailey. It's me, Ellie. I, um, well, I have something to tell you."

• • ○ • • • • • • • ❤ •

On Monday morning, Ellie got dressed and dragged herself down to breakfast. "Has Hailey called back?" she asked her mom.

Her mom shook her head no. "Not yet," she said gently.

At school, Ellie told her friends about her awful weekend. "First, we didn't find anyone to adopt Lulu. And then . . ." She cringed. "You guys, I really messed up."

She told them about the paint mishap.

"Can a flower girl get fired?" she asked them. "I feel like I might."

Her friends rallied around her. "It was an accident," Liz said. "Accidents happen."

"Yeah," Amy added. "Hailey will understand."

Ellie shrugged. "I don't know," she said uncertainly. "She hasn't called me back. Maybe it's because she's too mad to speak to me."

A Surprise Visitor

After school Ellie asked her mom again. "Has Hailey called?"

But she hadn't. She didn't call Monday evening. Or Tuesday morning. Or Tuesday after school, either. With each passing hour, Ellie was more and more sure: Hailey was furious with her.

The next day after school, Ellie and the girls were at The Critter Club. They were getting ready to walk both dogs—Lulu and Rufus, Ms. Sullivan's dog.

The dogs were outside the barn, playing. Tiny Lulu only came up to Rufus's knees. But both their tails wagged excitedly as they jumped around and barked loudly.

So Ellie did not hear Hailey arrive and walk up behind her. "Hi, Ellie," Hailey said. "Hi, girls."

Ellie whirled around, startled. She gulped.

Oh no! Hailey had come to fire her! Instead of calling her back, she had come to tell her face-to-face!

"Hailey!" Ellie cried out. "You're here!" Hailey opened her mouth to speak. But Ellie continued. "Wait," she said. "It's okay. You don't have to say it. I know why you're here."

Hailey looked surprised.

"You do?" she asked. "How?"

Ellie shrugged. "I just had a feeling," she replied.

Hailey nodded. "Connor and I have talked it over a lot. And we really feel this is the right thing to do."

Ellie felt tears welling up in her eyes. She

was so sad that Hailey and Connor didn't want her to be in their wedding anymore.

But Hailey looked pretty cheerful. "It's a big decision!" she said. "But we're excited about it!"

Whoa! Ellie thought. *That kind of hurt my feelings.* "Excited about it?" Ellie cried. "Really? Excited to replace me with a different flower girl?"

Hailey stared. "A different flower girl?" she repeated in disbelief. "Ellie! What are you talking about?"

Ellie frowned now too. "Wait.

What are *you* talking about?" Ellie asked.

Hailey threw up her hands. "I'm talking about adopting Lulu!" she exclaimed. "Connor and I want to adopt Lulu!"

Ellie Comes Clean

Marion, Amy, and Liz had over-
heard the whole thing. They gathered around Hailey, buzzing over
the big news.

"Lulu, did you hear that?" Liz
was saying.

"We have some questions to ask
you," Marion was telling Hailey.
"Just to make sure you and Lulu

are a good match."

Amy added, "But I bet you will be! Oh, this is so great!"

Meanwhile, Ellie's head was spinning. She was so surprised and happy for Lulu—and Hailey! But she was completely confused.

"Hailey," she said, "did you get my message?"

"Which message?" Hailey asked. "On my cell phone?" She sighed. "It's broken. I dropped it the other day. Now it won't

even turn on. I'm
sorry, Ellie. I didn't
get it." They sat down
side by side on the bench
by the maple tree. It was
the same bench where Hailey
had asked Ellie to be her flower girl.

"So what *was* your message?"

Ellie's shoulders slumped. She had to tell the whole terrible story *again*! This time to Hailey's face!

Before she lost her nerve, Ellie blurted it all out as fast as she could.

"Oh Hailey, I feel awful. I was trying on the flower girl dress. And there was this

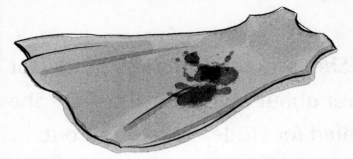

bottle of orange paint that I kind of squashed and the paint came squirting out and it got on the dress! So I showed my mom and she scraped some of it off, but we weren't sure whether we should try to wash it or not. And anyway, I called you to tell you what happened and to say I'm so, so, so sorry for messing up the dress."

Ellie took a deep breath. There. It was done.

She searched Hailey's face for clues about *how* mad she was. She waited for Hailey to let it all out.

But Hailey didn't. She just reached over and pulled Ellie into a big hug.

"Ellie," she said, "did you actually think I'd be mad? I understand. It was an accident. And we'll figure something out. Okay?"

Ellie beamed and sighed with relief. It felt like a huge weight had been lifted off her. "Hailey, you are the best!" Ellie exclaimed.

The two of them headed off to Ellie's house so Hailey could see the dress. Hailey scratched at the paint, which was dry and crusty.

She dabbed at it—
first with water,
then detergent,
and even a bit
of nail polish
remover. But the
stain wasn't going
anywhere.

Hailey looked up at Ellie.
"Well," she said, "we might to have
to try something different. Luckily,
I'm pretty handy with a needle and
thread. How about you?"

Ellie nodded. "I took a sewing
class last summer," she pointed out.

Hailey smiled and gave Ellie a thumbs-up. "Great," she said. "Because we're about to get creative."

The Big Day

Ellie and the bridesmaids were waiting by the rose arbor that led into the botanical garden. The wedding guests were all seated in the courtyard. The ceremony was set to begin. All they needed was the bride.

Then a shiny white car pulled up. Hailey and her parents got out.

Arm in arm, they walked over to the rose arbor.

Hailey's gown was a dreamy mix of silk and lace. Her hair was pinned up with pearl hairpins. And the veil! It trailed behind her as she walked.

"You look so beautiful!" Ellie said to Hailey.

But best of all, Hailey looked so happy. She smiled and gave Ellie a kiss on the cheek. "You look beautiful too!" Hailey replied.

"Thank you," Ellie said with a smile.

She loved her dress. Hailey had come up with such a clever idea. She had cut away the stained section of the skirt. Together, she and Ellie had hemmed the cut edges. Then Hailey had sewn in a white underskirt and something called a crinoline. It turned the skirt from a fitted one into a fuller, layered, flouncy one. Ellie thought that it twirled beautifully when she spun around.

They also added a pretty white belt with a fabric flower. It matched Ellie's white ballet flats and the white basket that held her flower petals.

Somehow, amazingly, the dress looked even better than the original!

Ellie could hear the music start-ing. It was almost time!

Suddenly, Ellie realized she was missing something. Or rather, some*one*.

Arf! Arf!

Lulu scurried out from behind the skirt of Hailey's dress. She was wearing a pink collar around her neck. Her leash was decorated with tiny flowers.

"Awww," Ellie said, kneeling down to pet Lulu. She took the leash from Hailey's dad, Uncle Walter. "You look so cute, Lulu!"

It had been Hailey's idea that Ellie walk Lulu down the aisle. Ellie loved the idea.

Ellie found her spot in line. She was right in front of Hailey and behind Toby, who was behind the bridesmaids.

"I'm so glad we found you a home!" Ellie said to Lulu.

Behind her, Hailey said, "I'm so glad her home is with us!"

Ellie took a deep breath. It was almost their turn to go. "Are you ready, Lulu?" she asked. "Ready for our big moment?"

Arf! Arf! Lulu replied.

Read on for a sneak peek at
the next Critter Club book:

#15

Liz's Night at
the Museum

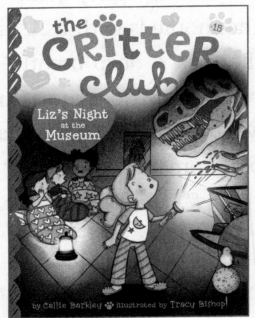

Liz Jenkins turned on her flashlight. She held it up to her chin so it illuminated just her face.

It was silent and shadowy in Liz's bedroom. Her best friends, Ellie, Amy, and Marion, waited for Liz to begin her story.

"It was a dark and stormy night," Liz said in a low voice.

"Uh-oh," said Amy. She pulled her sleeping bag up to her nose. "I don't like the sound of this."

Ellie giggled. "Stormy nights are always the spookiest!"

Marion yawned. "I think I've heard this one before," she said sleepily.

"Outside, lightning flashed," Liz continued. "Thunder clapped. But inside one house, four girls were having a sleepover."

"Just like us!" Ellie whispered.

Liz went on. "They were all in their sleeping bags. One of the girls had just finished telling a story. It was a scary story about a ghost, with rattling, clattering footsteps roaming her house at night."

Now Amy's sleeping bag was covering her head. She let out a squeak from inside.

"Don't worry," Marion gently told Amy. "It's just a story."

Liz suddenly flicked off her flashlight. The bedroom went completely dark.

"All of a sudden, one of the girls gasped," Liz went on. "'What was that?' the girl cried. The others listened. They heard it too!" Liz stomped her foot on the ground. "*Thwump—rattle. Thwump—rattle.* Rattling, clattering footsteps! Coming from the other side of the bedroom door!"

Marion sat up straight. "Shhh!" she said, suddenly wide-awake. "Did you hear that?"

Liz looked confused. "Hear what?" she replied. Then she smiled. "Oooh. Nice one, Marion. Trying to scare the storyteller."

Marion shook her head. Her eyes were wide in alarm. "No. Listen!"

The four girls sat silently, listening.

They all heard it. *Thwump— rattle. Thwump—rattle. Thwump— rattle.* Each time it was a little louder.

"Rattling, clattering footsteps!" Liz whispered.

"Coming closer," Ellie said shakily.

Amy stayed hidden inside her sleeping bag. "Is it coming from the hallway?" she asked.

Liz flicked her flashlight back on. She aimed the beam at her bedroom door. Liz, Ellie, and Marion watched it, trying not to blink.

Thwump—rattle. Thwump—rattle. Louder and louder, until . . .

Silence.

And then, slowly, Liz's doorknob turned.

the CRitter club

Join the club!

THE MOST IMPORTANT
DECISION YOU WILL EVER MAKE